Weekly Reader Children's Book Club presents

Mouse Trouble

story by
John Yeoman
pictures by
Quentin Blake

The Macmillan Company, New York, New York

A long, long time ago there stood an old windmill, perched on the top of a hill. In its day it had been a very fine windmill, but the miller who owned it now was a mean, bad-tempered man, who would never spend money on repairs. There was one thing that made him especially grumpy—mouse trouble.

There were hundreds of mice in the old mill
and they loved it there. They didn't mind
the noise of the creaking machinery, grinding
away. They had a marvelous time using
the great millstone as a merry-go-round...

...balancing on
    the turning beams...

...and sliding down
    the grain chutes.

They were so happy in the mill that often, on clear
moonlit nights, when the sails had stopped turning
and the machinery was still, they would form a circle
around their leader—a white mouse who had escaped
from a pet shop—and tell mouse jokes and sing songs
in their high twittery voices.

Although he never saw the mice, the grumpy miller knew they were there by their footprints, and the nibbled sacks, and the twittery singing in the dark.

And so he bought a large tabby cat
to help solve his mouse problem.

But the miller was so mean that he wouldn't give the cat
anything to eat and used to kick him, too. As a result
the cat moped about, worrying because he knew he wasn't
lively enough to catch any of those frisky mice.

The mice, though, felt rather sorry for the tabby and were unhappy to see him looking so down in the mouth. The white mouse called a meeting.

"That cat needs more exercise," he said. "We must make it easier for him to chase us."

"What good will that do?" asked a fat little piebald mouse.

"It will make him livelier and happier—and it will provide us with some good games," said the white mouse.

At this they all twittered with delight.

And so they began to make life more exciting
for him. Sometimes they sat on the turning sails
and made rude faces at him when they glided
past his favorite seat at the window.

Sometimes they covered him with flour dust
that had settled on the ledges and shelves.
Sometimes the younger mice let the tabby see them
and chase them. And they always pretended
to be terrified of him, so that he'd have
something to feel proud about.

And, sure enough, it all began to have an effect on
the tabby. He started to take a pride in himself.
One day the white mouse sat watching him practice
in front of a broken mirror in the shed.

First he practiced slinking up to a screwdriver
as though it were a mouse.

Then he practiced pouncing on it ferociously.

And then he practiced being thanked
by the grateful miller.

The white mouse enjoyed this immensely and said
aloud, in his best quivery voice, "Oh, bless my soul,
what a terrifying cat! I feel quite faint."
And with that he scampered off.

As the cat grew livelier, the mice became even happier.
Every night, while the cat slept soundly after his efforts
to keep the mice in order, they all came out to celebrate.
Swarms of the younger ones would scuttle up and down
the ladder staircases with squeaks of delight, while the
older ones sat in the pockets of the workmen's aprons
hanging on the wall and looked on contentedly.
They thought how much nicer the world had become
since their young days.

One day, when the white mouse and two
of his friends were sitting on some sacks
of corn at the top of the mill, nibbling
newspapers into tiny pieces, they heard
a terrible shouting below.
They peered down the stairs and saw the
angry miller holding the poor tabby
by the scruff of his neck.
Above the swish of the sails and the
rumble of the machinery they heard him
shout: "You useless great thing! Since
I bought you there have been more mice
than ever. Very well. I'm going to put you
in a sack and tonight I'll take you to
the river and throw you in."

The mice were very upset and begged the white mouse
to do something. So, as soon as it was safe, he led a crowd
of them into the shed where the miller had taken the cat.
The wretched animal was already tied up in a sack, so the
white mouse climbed onto what he imagined was the cat's
shoulder and whispered into what was probably the cat's ear.

"My fellow mice," he whispered, "ask me to say that
although you are our dreaded enemy, we don't want you
to be drowned. If we help you to escape, will you promise
to be friends with us afterward?"
The poor trembling bundle nodded its head.
"Right," said the white mouse, and he gave out instructions.

One group, led by the white mouse, crept into the
hallway of the mill and quietly unhooked the miller's
wife's fur cape from its peg.

Carrying it above their heads,
they scampered back to the shed.

When they got there, another group had already
nibbled through the string which was tied round the
sack, and the cat was free and panting with relief.

In no time some of the mice stuffed the fur cape with straw, while some particularly strong ones dragged along a horseshoe so that they could make the sack heavier.

Then they filled the sack and tied it up again.
"That stupid miller will never know the difference," said the white mouse.

That night the miller took his sack down the lane
to the river, followed—although he didn't know it—
by hundreds of inquisitive mice.

They sat on the wall of the bridge and watched him fling the bundle into the water with a great splash. "That's the last we'll see of him," said the miller with a snort. And he set off for home with the mice silently following him again.

The miller decided that cats were no use
and he never bought another one.
But he didn't know that the great tabby,
still alive and much more contented than
he'd ever been, was living with the mice
on the very top floor of the mill, eating
all the best tidbits they could find
for him in the larder...

...and playing endless games
of cat and mouse.